Bat's Nap

and

Hip Hop Hat

By Cath Jones

Illustrated by
Diego Vaisburg

The Letter N

Trace the lower and upper case letter with a finger. Sound out the letter.

Down,
up,
around,
down

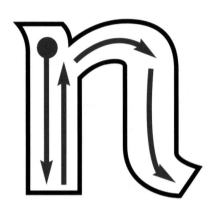

Down,
up,
down,
up

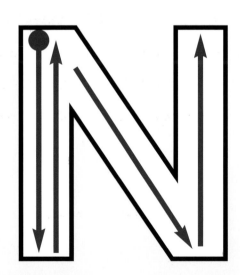

Some words to familiarise:

Bat   bell   rope

High-frequency words:

a   the

Tips for Reading 'Bat's Nap'

- Practise the words listed above before reading the story.

- If the reader struggles with any of the other words, ask them to look for sounds they know in the word. Encourage them to sound out the words and help them read the words if necessary.

- After reading the story, ask the reader why Bat is grumpy.

Fun Activity

Discuss other places that bats can sleep.

Bat's Nap

Bat can see a bell.

Bat can see a bed.

Cat can see Bat.

Cat can see a rope.

Bat can see
the rope.

15

Bat can nap.

Cat can nap.

The Letter H

Trace the lower and upper case letter with a finger. Sound out the letter.

*Down,
up,
around,
down*

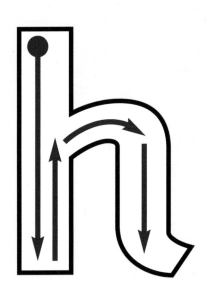

*Down,
lift
down,
lift,
cross*

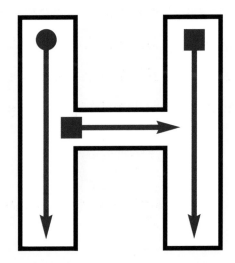

Some words to familiarise:

hat   show   bug

High-frequency words:

on a put

Tips for Reading 'Hip Hop Hat'

- Practise the words listed above before reading the story.

- If the reader struggles with any of the other words, ask them to look for sounds they know in the word. Encourage them to sound out the words and help them read the words if necessary.

- After reading the story, ask the reader why Bug wanted a hat.

Fun Activity

Discuss some other musical hats that the animals could wear!

Hip Hop Hat

Put on a hat.

Cat put on a hat.

Bat put on a hat.

25

Hen put on a hat.

Cat, Bat and Hen put on a show.

Bug put on a hat.

Book Bands for Guided Reading

Pink

Red

Yellow

Blue

Green

Orange

Turquoise

Purple

Gold

White

The Institute of Education book banding system is a scale of colours that reflects the various levels of reading difficulty. The bands are assigned by taking into account the content, the language style, the layout and phonics. Word, phrase and sentence level work is also taken into consideration.

Maverick Early Readers are a bright, attractive range of books covering the pink to white bands. All of these books have been book banded for guided reading to the industry standard and edited by a leading educational consultant.

To view the whole Maverick Readers scheme, visit our website at

www.maverickearlyreaders.com

Or scan the QR code above to view our scheme instantly!